Magic Animal Friends

For Eddie, my breakfast buddy
with love

Special thanks to Valerie Wilding

ORCHARD BOOKS
338 Euston Road, London NW1 3BH
Orchard Books Australia
Level 17/207 Kent Street, Sydney, NSW 2000
A Paperback Original

First published in 2015 by Orchard Books

A CIP catalogue record for this book is available
from the British Library.

ISBN 978 1 40834 846 8

5 7 9 8 6

Printed and bound in Great Britain by Clays Ltd, Elcograf S.p.A.

FSC www.fsc.org MIX Paper from responsible sources FSC® C104740

The paper and board used in this book are made from wood
from responsible sources.

Orchard Books is a division of Hachette Children's Books,
an Hachette UK company.

www.hachette.co.uk

Sophie Flufftail's Brave Plan

Daisy Meadows

ORCHARD

Sunshine Meadow
Shining House
Blossom Briar
Toadstool Cafe
Goldie's Grotto
Toadstool Glade
Mrs Taptree's Library
Library
Friendship Tree
Maze
Silver Spring
Buttercup Grove
Lighthouse

Map of Friendship Forest

Can you keep a secret? I thought you could!

Then I'll tell you about an enchanted wood.

It lies through the door in the old oak tree,

Let's go there now - just follow me!

We'll find adventure that never ends,

And meet the Magic Animal Friends!

Love

Goldie the Cat

Contents

CHAPTER ONE: A Stormy Day	9
CHAPTER TWO: Back to Friendship Forest	23
CHAPTER THREE: Grizelda's Plan	33
CHAPTER FOUR: Chilly's Icy Spell	49
CHAPTER FIVE: Little Lola	59
CHAPTER SIX: Hotpots	67
CHAPTER SEVEN: Inside the Winter Cave	81
CHAPTER EIGHT: Sunshine	95

CHAPTER ONE

A Stormy Day

Jess Forester smiled as she spread some sunshine-yellow butter on her last piece of crusty bread. "That was a lovely lunch, Dad," she said.

"Mmm," said her best friend, Lily Hart. "Cheese, chutney and walnuts. Yum!"

Mr Forester smiled. "Have some more

nuts. We picked lots before the squirrels took them all."

"If I eat any more nuts, I'll turn into a squirrel!" Jess joked, getting up to clear the table. "Anyway, we've got to get back to Helping Paw."

The two girls smiled at each other.

They were lucky to live on the same road – and even luckier that Lily's parents ran the Helping Paw Wildlife Hospital. The hospital looked after all kinds of animals in need, and both Jess and Lily loved helping there whenever they could!

Mr Forester glanced out of the window. "Take your coats," he said. "It looks like it's about to rain, and you don't want to get wet."

As he spoke, rain splattered against the window. Jess and Lily put their coats and wellies on and Jess picked up her big rainbow-striped umbrella.

When they stepped outside, Lily's dark bobbed hair blew across her face. She ducked under Jess's umbrella and glanced at her friend. "The rain's making your hair curlier than ever!" she smiled.

Once they'd crossed the lane, Jess opened Lily's gate and ran down to the Helping Paw barn at the bottom of the garden.

But as she raced after her friend,

Lily spotted something strange beneath the chestnut tree. "Wait!" she cried.

Lily showed Jess a heap of leaves and twigs. "Something's moving under there," she whispered.

Lily pushed the wet leaves aside. Underneath were three bright-eyed creatures huddled together, long tails curling round their tiny, furry bodies.

Lily gasped. "Baby squirrels!" she cried. "They must have fallen from the tree." She glanced around. There was no sign of the babies' parents anywhere.

"They're so tiny," said Jess, moving

her umbrella to shelter the little squirrels from the rain. "We can't leave them here. They're already soaked."

"You're right," said Lily. "Mum and Dad say you should usually leave baby animals alone, in case their parents come looking for them, but I think we have to take them to the wildlife hospital." She scooped up two baby squirrels, and Jess gently picked up the third.

When they reached the barn, Lily knocked on the door with her foot.

Mrs Hart opened it. "Goodness!" she exclaimed when she saw the squirrels. "Bring them in!"

Lily and Jess carried the babies to Mr Hart, who was standing by the examination table. The girls gently put them on the table, then as they took off their coats and wellies they explained where they'd found them.

Mrs Hart found a nest box, and Lily cut some squares of soft blanket to line it.

These will make a cosy bed," she said.

"Like a proper squirrel home!" said Jess. "Nice and warm and dry."

They gently lifted in the three babies, while Mr and Mrs Hart went to the kitchen area to find them some food.

Lily and Jess were watching the little squirrels snuggle up to each other cosily, when they heard something tapping at the barn window.

They looked up to see a beautiful green-eyed cat on the sill outside. Raindrops sparkled on her whiskers.

"Goldie!" whispered Jess.

"She's drenched!" said Lily, flying to open the window.

The cat darted inside and jumped down, her fur dripping on the floor.

Jess leapt up to fetch a towel. Excitement fizzed through her as she gently dried the cat's golden fur. Goldie might look like an ordinary cat, but Jess and Lily shared a wonderful secret – Goldie lived in Friendship Forest, a magical world filled with talking animals!

Goldie purred as the girls patted her dry.

"Maybe Friendship Forest is in danger again," wondered Lily out loud.

"I hope Grizelda isn't back," said Jess anxiously.

Grizelda was a wicked witch who wanted to take Friendship Forest all for herself. She had sent the Boggits, her four smelly servants, into the forest to ruin it. Luckily, the girls and Goldie had managed to stop Grizelda's plan and save the forest.

Goldie looked up and mewed, then padded over to the door.

"She wants us to follow her!" said Jess. Her blue eyes shone. "Lily, I think Goldie's going to take us back to Friendship Forest!"

"We're going to see our animal friends again!" said Lily, smiling. She jumped up and peered out of the window. Luckily the rain had stopped. "Mum!" she called to Mrs Hart. "We're going outside."

"OK," called Mrs Hart.

Pulling their coats and wellies on, the girls followed Goldie past Helping Paw and down to Brightley Stream. They hopped across the stepping stones and ran towards the tree in the middle of Brightley Meadow. It looked like a dead oak tree, but the girls knew that it was the Friendship Tree, and it was very special.

Lily and Jess ran up to the tree and grinned at each other. Something magical was about to happen!

As Goldie reached the tree, leaves sprang from the lifeless branches, birds swooped down to sing sweet songs, and brilliant butterflies danced above the bright yellow flowers that bloomed below. Lily ran her fingers over two words carved into the tree's bark. "Ready, Jess?" she asked, feeling a thrill of excitement.

Together they read the words aloud, "Friendship Forest!"

Instantly a door with a leaf-shaped handle appeared in the trunk. Jess clasped Lily's hand and opened the door. Shimmering light shone from inside. They ducked and followed Goldie into the golden glow.

What magical adventure would they have this time? Lily and Jess couldn't wait to find out!

CHAPTER TWO

Back to Friendship Forest

As the golden light surrounded them, Jess and Lily tingled all over as they magically shrank. Then the light faded and they were in Friendship Forest once more. A warm breeze drifted past, catching the lemon and chocolate scents of the flowers growing around them. It was so different from the rainy day in Brightley that it was easy to tell that they were in a magical world!

"Welcome back," said a soft voice.

They turned to see Goldie, but she didn't look like an ordinary cat at all any more. She was standing on her back legs, with a glittering golden scarf wrapped around her shoulders. She smiled and the girls rushed over to hug her.

"It's lovely to be back," cried Jess.

"And to talk to you again," said Lily.

"But why have you brought us here

today, Goldie?" Jess asked her.

Goldie twitched her tail anxiously. "Come and see what's happened in Sunshine Meadow."

"Wait," said Lily, tugging at her coat. "It's so lovely and warm here that we don't need these!" They took off their raincoats and stowed them at the foot of the Friendship Tree.

As they set off with Goldie, they passed lots of gorgeous tiny cottages nestled among tree roots and up in the tree branches. It was a perfect little village – for all kinds of amazing animals!

A scrummy baking smell wafted from the windows of a pretty cottage perched on a branch overhead. The door opened and a mouse in an apron scurried out. "Hello, Jess and Lily!" she cried.

"Hi, Mrs Twinkletail!" the girls called.

Lily smiled at Jess. "I still can't quite believe that we can talk to all the animals here! It's wonderful!"

They hurried on to Toadstool Glade. Agatha Glitterwing the magpie was

busy

chatting

to Mr Silverback

the badger, while a

group of young animals

played with a skipping rope made of flowers. Outside the Toadstool Café, the Prickleback hedgehog family were sipping delicious-looking drinks. Everyone waved happily at Lily and Jess as they passed by.

Jess and Lily waved back, but there was no time to stop. Goldie was bounding ahead, her tail twitching anxiously.

"Poor Goldie seems really worried," Jess whispered to Lily as they hurried after their friend. "Something really bad must have happened."

When they reached Sunshine Meadow, both girls gasped in horror.

Huge patches of the red, yellow and orange flowers that grew there were scorched and blackened.

"Oh no!" Lily exclaimed. "Who would burn the beautiful flowers?"

Goldie's whiskers drooped sadly. "It's terrible, isn't it?" she sniffed.

"Maybe it was the Boggits?" Jess wondered out loud.

The Boggits were hairy, smelly creatures who had been Grizelda's servants until Jess and Lily had found them a new home in the stinky swamp.

"No, it's not them." Goldie shook her head. "They're friendly now they have their swampy home."

"Don't worry, Goldie," Jess began. "We'll—" She froze as a familiar orb of yellow-green light suddenly floated across the meadow towards them.

"It's Grizelda!" cried Lily.

With a *cra-ack* the orb burst into a shower of evil-smelling sparks, which cleared to reveal the witch in a black cloak, purple tunic and trousers. Her green hair swirled like angry snakes as she stamped her pointy-toed boot.

Goldie took a brave step towards her. "Stay away from Friendship Forest, Grizelda!" she cried.

The witch cackled. "Ha! It's the cat and the meddlesome girls," she spat. "But who cares? I'm going to make Friendship

Forest so horrible that no one will want to live in it. Then I'll have it all for myself!"

Lily and Jess stepped beside Goldie. "No, you won't," shouted Jess. "We won't let you!"

Grizelda gave another horrible laugh. "You can't stop me this time," she said. I have new servants to carry out my plan – magical ones. They're far better than Boggits!"

She clapped once and pointed into the sky, where four winged creatures were flying towards them.

Goldie's green eyes were wide. "What are those?"

"They're too big for birds," said Lily.

"They can't be bats," said Jess. "Not with those long tails."

"But what else flies?" Goldie said. "I can't think—"

They all gasped as one of the creatures let a stream of fire out of its mouth.

"Dragons!" both girls squealed together.

CHAPTER THREE

Grizelda's Plan

Lily, Jess and Goldie huddled together as the four dragons hovered around Grizelda. They were almost as big as the girls and all different colours: one red, one blue, one yellow and one black.

The red dragon nipped at Grizelda's long green hair as he flew past.

"Stop it, Breezy," snapped the witch, batting her out of the way.

The red dragon twisted over and over through the air as he flew.

The yellow one giggled so much that she hiccupped. A whoosh of fire shot from her mouth, scorching another patch of flowers to a crisp.

Lily and Jess exchanged

a glance. Now they knew who'd been ruining Sunshine Meadow!

"Dragons," said Grizelda, "meet two interfering nuisances and their irritating pet cat."

"She's not our pet!" Jess shouted. "She's Goldie, and she's wise, clever, brave and beautiful."

"My servants are cleverer than any cat!" Grizelda screeched. "And they can do more than breathe fire. Dragons!" Grizelda stomped her foot and the four dragons all jumped. "Show them!"

The red dragon swooped down. "I'm Breezy the storm dragon. I can make WIND!" She beat her wings and a blast of wind blew Jess and Lily's hair backwards.

Next the black dragon hovered over them, casting a dark shadow. "I'm Smudge," he said. "I can make inky darkness."

The giggly yellow dragon said, "I'm Dusty. I could turn you to stone. Tee hee!"

They all turned to look at the blue dragon, who was turning in lazy circles high in the sky.

"Show them your power, Chilly!" shouted Grizelda.

"Shan't," said the dragon. He stuck out his tongue at the witch.

Grizelda pointed a bony finger and a

jet of sparks shot past his tail. He jumped. "Ow! I hate hot things!"

"I know!" Grizelda sneered.

Jess and Lily glanced at each other. Grizelda was even horrible to her own servants!

"I'm Chilly," the dragon said, scowling. He blew a puff of snowflakes. "I make things cold."

"These dragons," said Grizelda, "will help me with my brilliant new plan!" Her dark eyes glittered. "It's sunshine that makes Friendship Forest all green and flowery," she sneered. "Urgh! Green is for hair, not leaves! I'll get rid of the sunshine so Friendship Forest turns dark and cold and all the plants will die."

Jess, Lily and Goldie looked at each other in dismay.

"Then the animals will leave and then the forest will be all mine!" screeched Grizelda.

She snapped her fingers and disappeared, along with the dragons, in a burst of stinking yellow sparks.

Goldie's eyes swam with tears. "She'll destroy our beautiful forest," she said. "We must stop her!"

"But how?" said Lily. "We don't know what's she's planning to do."

"How can she get rid of the sunshine?" Jess wondered out loud.

Goldie gasped. "Of course! Grizelda's going to attack the Shining House!"

"What's the Shining House?" Lily asked.

"I'll show you," said Goldie. "It's on the far side of Sunshine Meadow. Follow me!"

"It's amazing!" Lily gasped as she and Jess gazed at a beautiful glasshouse. Sunlight sparkled off every pane, and a beautiful heart-shaped diamond glittered and shone in the roof.

"Wow!" they breathed.

"It keeps the whole of Friendship Forest bright and warm," Goldie explained. "Without it, everywhere would be cold and dark."

"Just what Grizelda wants!" Jess said with a frown.

"Hello!" A little squirrel in a spotty T-shirt bounded up to them.

"Woody!" Jess smiled, bending to hug him. They'd met the young squirrel on their adventures before.

"We need your help." Lily told him gently. "We think Grizelda is going to attack the Shining House!"

Woody gasped, his bushy tail shivering in fear. "Come and see Mum and Dad," he said, taking them inside.

The Shining House was full of yellow sunflowers, and every sunflower face was turned towards the sun. The air shimmered with a magical golden glow.

Two big squirrels were busy high up on the roof, polishing the glass with their long, fluffy tails. Three small squirrels were working just as hard polishing the inside.

Swish! Swish! Swish!

The two big squirrels waved through the glass roof.

"Hello, Mr and Mrs Flufftail!" Jess and Lily called up to them.

"This is my brother Dasha," explained Woody, "and my big sisters, Hazel and Lulu."

A tiny squirrel wearing a stripy T-shirt peeked out from behind Woody.

"And this is Sophie," Woody said. "She's the youngest Flufftail."

"Hi!" said Sophie, waving at the girls with her tail.

"Hi, Sophie!" said Lily. "It's lovely to meet you all."

"Flufftails, we need your help," Jess said urgently. "We think Grizelda is going to cause trouble here. Can you tell us how the Shining House works?"

"Of course," Mr Flufftail scurried down from the roof and over to them. "The trees have so many beautiful green leaves that the sun can't shine through them all to reach the forest floor," he explained, pointing at the trees with his tail. "So the Shining House collects the light. Then the sunflowers magically reflect the sunshine through the glass and out into the forest, to make the whole forest lovely and light and warm."

"We keep the glass polished," Woody said proudly. "Only a Flufftail fluff tail is soft enough to clean the Shining House. Feel!" he added, flicking his tail out towards her.

Lily stroked his beautiful bushy tail. It felt as soft as silk. "It's gorgeous," she said.

"Do you really think Grizelda is going to come here?" Woody asked sadly.

"Don't worry, we'll stop her," Jess said firmly.

"We've done it before and we'll do it again!" Lily agreed.

But just then the air turned icy cold. There was a whoosh and a cloud of snowflakes blew over them.

Jess heard wings flapping and looked up. "Oh no! It's Chilly the ice dragon!"

CHAPTER FOUR

Chilly's Icy Spell

"Dragon?" shrieked Mrs Flufftail. "Children, hide!"

The young Flufftails scattered. Woody and Dasha ran squealing behind Lily and Jess, and Hazel and Lulu hid under Mr Flufftail's tail.

As Chilly swooped down to land, he

blew a big raspberry, scattering ice flakes everywhere. "*Pffffttthh!*" he said. "I'm going to make the forest lovely and cold!"

"No!" cried Jess.

But Chilly pointed his wings at the Flufftails and chanted:

"Magic make these squirrels change
So they hate the golden sun
Then wintry cold will chill the trees
And bring snow for everyone."

For a moment, nothing seemed to happen. Then Goldie gasped. "Look at the

Flufftails!" she cried.

The squirrel family were curling their tails over their eyes.

"Too bright," they moaned.

"The sunshine's horrible," Woody said with a groan.

Chilly grinned, flicking icicles from his tail.

"Change the squirrels back to normal," Jess demanded.

"Won't!" said

Chilly and stuck out his tongue. He beat his wings again.

Instantly, an icy wind blew over the Shining House, and Chilly flew up into the sky, high above the treetops.

As the dragon flew away, the Flufftails disappeared into the woods, still covering their eyes.

"Wait!" Jess called, "Woody! Hazel! The poor Flufftails," she sighed as she turned to Lily and Goldie.

But Lily and Goldie were staring at the Shining House in dismay. The gleaming glass was covered with frost so thick that they could barely see inside. The sunflowers were already drooping in the cold. Worst of all, no light was shining out into the forest.

Goldie gave an upset sniffle.

"Everything will be fine," Jess promised. "We won't give up until it is."

"I know you won't," said Goldie. Her whiskers lifted a little.

There was a crackle from the bushes next to the Shining House.

"Someone's coming!" whispered Jess. "Careful, it might be Grizelda."

The girls held their breath. But instead

of Grizelda, little Sophie Flufftail crept out from behind a bush. She was trembling and looked very upset.

Lily knelt down. "It's OK, Sophie," she said. "The dragon's gone."

Sophie ran to Lily, who scooped her up, stroking the little squirrel's silky orange fur.

"I hid behind the bush when the dragon came," she told them. "Now my family have all got a spell put on them! I wish I'd come out and helped them." She burst into tears.

"There wasn't anything you could have done," Lily told her gently.

Jess stroked the trembling squirrel. "Don't worry, Sophie," she said. "We'll help your family."

"Really?" sniffed Sophie. She wiped her eyes with her tail.

Goldie nodded. "Of course we will. Lily and Jess always help animals in trouble."

"Thank you!" cried Sophie. She wriggled down from Lily's arms. "But first I've got to fix the Shining House."

She scampered over to it and rubbed the frosty glass with her tail. As soon as her bushy tail touched the glass, the frost started to fade. But even though she rubbed and rubbed, she only cleared a tiny patch of the glass.

Sophie's face fell. "I only have a little tail," she said sadly. "I can't polish it all on my own."

Everyone looked around the darkening forest anxiously. Without the Shining House, light was already fading away.

Jess turned to Goldie. "We need to lift Chilly's spell on the Flufftails so they can

all fix the Shining House. We've got to find them!"

"The spell has made them hate the sunshine," Lily said, "so maybe they've gone somewhere dark and cold. Goldie, do you know anywhere like that?"

Goldie shook her head.

"Then we'll just have to look for it," Jess said determinedly.

"We'll search the whole forest if we have to!" agreed Lily.

"OK," said Sophie. "Come on." She bounded ahead but stopped suddenly, jumping back in fright. A big mound of earth had simply popped out of the ground, right in front of her.

Another mound popped up nearby. Then another. And another!

Jess scooped up Sophie and huddled together with Goldie and Lily. "What's happening?" she whispered. "Is it more dragon magic?"

CHAPTER FIVE

Little Lola

"Stay back," Jess said, as another mound of earth appeared. "It could be Chilly, making more magic spells."

Pop! A fresh mound sprung up right by her foot. Suddenly a face appeared in the middle of the mound! It was a mole, wearing round purple-framed spectacles.

Goldie ran over, purring happily. "It's OK! Those mounds are molehills, and that's Lola Velvetnose!"

"Phew," said Lily, with a grin.

"Hello, Goldie!" Lola said, squinting up at them through her glasses. "Who's that next to you? She smells of honey!"

"This is Jess," said Goldie, going closer so the little mole could see her clearly. "She's a girl, and so is Lily."

Lola peered at Lily, then sniffed. "Mmm, you smell of strawberries," she said.

"You gave us a fright, making all those molehills!" Lily laughed.

"Sorry," said Lola. "I'm investigating a strange new scent underground – a strong smell of chestnuts."

"Oh!" cried Sophie, looking out from behind Lily. "That must be my family. We love chestnuts."

Lola's little pink nose went *woffle woffle*. "Yes," she said. "You smell of chestnuts, too."

"Are my family really underground?" Sophie asked.

"They must be," said Lola. "Follow me, everyone. I'll take you through one of my bigger tunnels."

She dug a hole wide enough for the girls, and they dropped down into a tunnel, followed by Goldie. Sophie cuddled into the crook of Lily's arm, her tail curled around her little body as she

held on tightly to her new friend.

The tunnel was cool and smelled of freshly dug earth, but as Lily stepped inside, it got darker and darker. "Wait!" she called as Lola scrabbled ahead. "We can't see!"

"I'll fix that," said Lola. She dug upwards, making a little hole that let in dim light and fresh air.

Everyone followed her until she stopped at a corner. *Woffle woffle* went her little pink nose.

"The chestnut smell is coming from somewhere nearby," she said.

They peered around the corner, and Sophie gave a little squeak.

At the end of the tunnel was an

underground cottage. Outside were several deck chairs. Mr Silverback the badger, wearing his green waistcoat, sat in one. And in the others were the Flufftails!

"Hello there!" called Mr Silverback in a rumbling voice. "Have you come to visit my underground garden, too?"

"Mum! Dad!" cried Sophie. She scurried over to them as the girls and Goldie explained to Mr Silverback what had happened.

"Dear me," he said, scratching his stripy head. "No wonder they keep complaining about the light."

"We're going to take you home," Sophie told her family.

"We can't go home," said Mr Flufftail. "The sun's shining. We don't like sunshine."

And they refused to move.

Sophie gave a little sob and Jess stroked her head comfortingly.

Goldie looked at the girls in dismay. "If we can't get the Flufftails to fix the Shining House, the forest will be dark and cold forever!"

CHAPTER SIX

Hotpots

"Let's go to the Toadstool Café to think." Jess suggested.

"Don't worry, young Sophie," said Mr Silverback. "Your family will be safe here with me."

They thanked the badger and Sophie hugged each member of her family goodbye. Lola dug upwards, making a hole big enough for everyone to climb out.

As the girls reached the surface, they stared around in shock. The forest was so different from the sunny place they'd seen when they'd stepped through the Friendship Tree. Without the Shining House it was gloomy and grey and the air was damp and cold.

"We have to fix this," Goldie said miserably.

"Can I come with you to the Toadstool Café?" asked Lola. "I don't want to meet

Chilly by myself."

"Of course," said Lily, holding the mole's soft paw comfortingly.

They walked back to Toadstool Glade. The café was full of shivering rabbits, cold birds and mice with chattering teeth, but they all squeezed in to make room.

"Everyone take one of my play cots – I mean clay pots," said a voice from somewhere in the middle of the room.

Jess grinned. "I know who that is!"

They made their way through the crowded café to where Mr Cleverfeather was handing out red-brown pots to all the shivering little animals.

"Hello," he said, when he saw Goldie and the girls. "Something's long with the forest, and everyone's sold – I mean, something's wrong and everyone's cold. So I invented these hotpots." He passed some over to Lily, Jess and Goldie.

The round pots felt smooth and warm. Jess peeked under the lid of her hotpot and saw softly glowing embers. The girls, Goldie and Sophie sat down and held the cosy pots. They felt even better when Mrs Longwhiskers came over with a tray of hot blackberry tea and blossom buns.

"Mmm," Lily sighed as she enjoyed the buns' gooey golden filling, which tasted like butterscotch.

"Yummy!" Jess agreed. She looked around at the animals all huddled together. "Right, what are we going to do? We need to fix the Shining House and the Flufftails can't help us."

All the animals leaned in to listen. "Maybe we could break Chilly's magic somehow?" Lily thought out loud.

Goldie glanced up as a long-legged stork wearing a flying helmet appeared through the crowd, carrying a tall cup made from bamboo. "Hello, Captain Ace," she said. "Have you ever met a dragon on any of your long flights?"

Captain Ace nodded. "I did once. Now that was a very interesting journey."

"Do you know anything about their magic?" asked Lily eagerly.

"One thing I know is that you can't lift a dragon's spell," said the captain. "You have to persuade the dragon to do it himself."

He dipped his beak into his tea as he strode away.

"If he's right," said Lily, "we must find Chilly."

"But where could he be?" Jess said.

Sophie shivered. "An ice dragon would probably go somewhere really cold."

Lola wriggled. "Ooh! I know! The Winter Cave."

Goldie's green eyes gleamed. "Lola, that sounds like exactly the right place! But where is it?"

"It's just beyond the Silver Spring," said Lola. "I tunnelled into it by mistake one day, and nearly froze! I'm never going there again."

"That must be it!" exclaimed Jess. "Lola, you don't have to come, but could you tell us how to find it?"

"It's very simple," the mole said. "Instead of going through the maze to the Silver Spring, you go around it. Look for a glowing bush and the cave entrance is just beneath."

"A glowing bush?" Goldie said in surprise. "I've never heard of one of those in Friendship Forest."

"At least it'll be easy to spot." Jess shrugged. "Come on!"

"I'll go back and tell the Flufftails not to worry," Lola volunteered.

The girls, Goldie and Sophie waved

goodbye to Lola and their other friends, and set off. But as Lily passed the Friendship Tree, she cried, "Stop!" and ran to grab the coats they'd left there. "Even with the hotpots, it's getting so cold that we might need these," she explained.

They put them on gladly.

"Hey, turn round, Lily," said Jess. She picked Sophie up and nestled her into Lily's fur-lined hood. The little squirrel curled her tail round her toes.

"Ooh, it's so snuggly," she said with a smile. "Thank you!"

On they went, clutching the hotpots,

which were still beautifully warm. At last, they saw a light up ahead.

"The glowing bush!" Lily laughed when she saw it.

"Poor Lola couldn't see – it isn't the bush that's glowing!" Jess giggled as she looked at the plant. It was covered with gorgeous fireflies, eating the leaves!

"And here's the entrance to the Winter Cave," Goldie said, pulling aside the leaves.

They'd only taken a few steps inside the cave when a rumbling noise echoed though the air. Lily, Jess and Goldie stopped, and Sophie ducked even further down into Lily's hood.

"What was that?" exclaimed Jess. "It sounded like horrible laughter."

"We have to keep going," said Lily with a gulp. She took another step forward, then gasped. "Come and look!" she whispered.

Jess and Goldie joined her. Sophie looked over Lily's shoulder as they all peered into the mouth of the cave.

"Wow!" said Lily.

It was dark inside the cave, but the walls, roof and floor shimmered with

gleaming ice. Long icicles hung from the roof and the rocks on the ground glittered with frost.

And in the middle, his tail over his eyes, and his body shaking, was Chilly. But he wasn't laughing...he was crying!

CHAPTER SEVEN

Inside the Winter Cave

Chilly whimpered again. With each cry, puffs of snow blew out from his mouth.

"What's wrong with him?" Jess asked.

"We have to help him," Lily said.

"But what if he puts a spell on us too?" said Goldie. "Then who will help the Flufftails and save Friendship Forest?"

Chilly gave a great rattling sniffle, then puffed out more snow.

Lily and Jess looked at each other. Goldie was right. What were they going to do? Before they could move, Lily's hood started wriggling. Sophie jumped out and darted down Lily's back.

"Sophie, no!" Jess whispered.

But Sophie didn't listen. "I hid before, but I'm not hiding any more!" she chattered as she jumped down on the floor of the Winter Cave, then bravely scampered over to the dragon.

"Take the spell off my family, you big

meanie!" she shouted as she scurried right up to Chilly and stood in front of him.

The crying stopped. The dragon's eyes snapped open and he jumped onto his clawed feet. Chilly opened his mouth, as if he was about to roar…

But to the girls' surprise, the little dragon gave another whimper.

"Who's there?" he asked, his scaly legs

trembling. "Are you a monster?"

Sophie looked shocked. "No, it's me, Sophie Flufftail," she told him. "And my friends. Why did you think we were monsters, Chilly?"

Chilly trembled. "Anything could be hiding in the dark."

"Chilly's scared of the dark!" Lily gasped. "That's why he was crying!"

"Of course!" said Jess. "The forest is colder and darker without the Shining House. Chilly likes how cold it is, but he doesn't like the darkness!"

Goldie's green eyes gleamed. "Clever

Sophie for talking to him! We'd never have realised, otherwise."

Lily glanced down at the hotpot in her hand. It had given her an idea. She lifted the lid, and a warm light shone out, making the icicles on the roof glitter like chandeliers.

Chilly gazed up, his eyes wide. "Oooh," he breathed happily.

Lily held the hotpot out to him.

"You can have it, if you want," she told him, "as long as you do something for us."

Chilly reached a scaly paw towards the hotpot. Then he leapt back. "Hot!" he roared angrily, blowing a puff of snow over them all.

Lily glanced anxiously at Jess and Goldie. What should they do now? Sophie scampered over and they all gathered on one side of the cave.

"If only the hotpot wasn't *hot*," Goldie sighed.

"We need one of Mr Cleverfeather's glow-worm lanterns," said Jess, thinking back on one of their other adventures. "They made light but they weren't too warm."

"Oh, I know!" cried Sophie. "There were fireflies outside. Maybe they'd light the cave for Chilly?"

Goldie ran outside as fast as her paws could take her.

"Chilly, we think we can make the Winter Cave nice and light," Jess said. "But we want you to do something in return. Will you take your spell off Sophie's family?"

"Can't," said Chilly.

"But why not?" Jess asked.

The little dragon shrugged sadly.

Jess remembered how bossy Grizelda was to the dragons when they first saw them in Brightley Meadow.

"Is it because of Grizelda?" she asked.

Chilly nodded his scaly blue head.

"You don't have to do what she says," Jess went on.

Chilly looked puzzled. "Don't I?"

"No," said Lily, catching on to what Jess was thinking. "Dragons don't take orders from witches!"

Chilly roared again, sending more snow

fluttering around the cave. "I'm going to lift my spell, whether she likes it or not! *Pffffftttt!*" He blew a huge raspberry.

Brave Sophie raced over to Chilly and gave him a hug. "Thank you!" she said.

The girls cheered. "Now we just need Goldie to get the fireflies to agree to help," Lily said.

"I don't think we need to worry about that," Jess smiled. "Look!"

Goldie rushed back into the cave, followed by a gorgeous fluttering cloud of golden fireflies.

"You must promise not to hurt the

fireflies, Chilly," Goldie told him sternly.

Chilly looked around happily. "Lovely light." He blew out a breath which sparkled with frost. Then he stared shyly at Sophie and the girls. "Thank you."

Lily smiled at the little dragon. Thanks to Sophie, they'd found out that he wasn't so bad after all. "You're welcome, Chilly. Now let's break that spell!"

Lola, the Flufftails and Mr Silverback gasped with surprise when the dragon peered down the hole down into the underground garden.

"Chilly's going to lift the spell so you'll love the sunshine again," Lily told the squirrels.

Chilly beat his wings and chanted,

"Dragon wings stop Chilly's spell
Grizelda's had her fun
Make squirrels be themselves again
And love the golden sun."

Instantly, the young Flufftails started squealing. "It's so dark!" squeaked Woody.

"Where are we?" asked Dasha.

"You've been under a spell that made you hate the sunshine," said Jess.

"We must get back home to the Shining House!" said Mr Flufftail. "Come along, children, quickly!"

Lola and Mr

Silverback helped them climb out of the tunnel, and Sophie quickly told her family the whole story. The Flufftails thanked everyone.

"As for you, Sophie," said her father, "you're the bravest little squirrel there ever was. We're so proud of you."

Everyone hugged, then Mrs Flufftail shivered. "Brrr! We'd better put the Shining House right before the forest becomes any more wintry." She bounded away. "Come on, Flufftails. Work to do!"

Goldie smiled. "When the Shining House is gleaming once more," she said,

"Then Grizelda's plan will have failed!"

Lily turned to Chilly. "Thank you for freeing them. You're not going to cast any more spells, are you?"

Chilly shook his head. "I'm going to play in the Winter Cave! The fireflies have made it so nice and light!"

The girls and Goldie waved as he flew a loop-the-loop over their heads, then flapped away. Goldie, Lily and Jess grinned, then raced after their squirrel friends. It was time to fix the Shining House for good!

CHAPTER EIGHT

Sunshine

Goldie and the girls found the whole squirrel family at the Shining House, lined up before Mr Flufftail.

"Ready, kids?" he said. "We'll get this glass gleaming in no time! Everyone fluff up your tails!"

The squirrels shook their tails until they

looked as soft and fluffy as dandelion clocks. Then they started to wipe the frost from the glass. *Swish! Swish! Swish!*

"We can't clean the glass," said Jess, "but is there another way we can help?"

"You could water the sunflowers," Sophie suggested.

Once the sunshine started streaming in and the sunflowers had been watered, they stood up straight and tilted their faces towards the sky.

In less than an hour, the Shining House was almost clean. As Sophie's tail rubbed away the last patch of frost, the sun came out from behind the clouds. Sunbeams shone on the sunflowers' upturned faces, then golden sunlight arched up through the beautifully polished glass.

Everyone gasped in delight and ran outside to feel the warmth of the sun streaming round the forest.

The squirrels linked tails and danced round and round, waving

their paws in the air happily.

The girls laughed, but Lily suddenly cried out, "Look!"

A familiar orb of light flew across Sunshine Meadow and exploded in a shower of sparks. When they cleared, there stood Grizelda.

"You interfering humans!" she shrieked. "You've ruined my plan!"

"It was a wicked plan," said Jess. "We had to stop you to save the forest and all the lovely creatures living in it!"

"Lovely creatures, pah!" screeched Grizelda. "You wait – you and that cat won't stop me next time. Chilly might have disobeyed me, but I have three more magical dragon servants. They won't let me down!"

She snapped her fingers, and disappeared in a burst of horrid, smelly yellow-green sparks.

The squirrels stared at each other in shock. Then Sophie bravely jumped forward and stuck her tongue out at where Grizelda used to be, making everyone laugh.

"Come on, you must be hungry after that adventure." Mrs Flufftail brought out a picnic box and soon they were all nibbling delicious home-made nut bread with hazelnut butter, and apricot pies.

When they'd all eaten it was time for Lily and Jess to go home. They said goodbye to the Flufftails, and gave Sophie an especially big hug.

"You're such a brave little squirrel," Lily whispered as she said goodbye.

As Goldie took them back to the Friendship Tree, Lily and Jess passed lots of their animal friends sitting and enjoying the sunshine.

"Look," said Goldie, pointing to a starflower bush. It was smothered in white buds. "Thanks to you, the flowers are blooming again. The Shining House is working its magic!"

When they reached the Friendship Tree, Goldie put a paw to the trunk and the door appeared. She hugged the girls.

"I expect Grizelda will think of another plan to drive us all out of the forest," she said. "After all, she's still got three more dragons. But I know I can count on you to help us again."

"Of course you can," said Jess.

"We'll be ready whenever you come for us," added Lily.

They stepped into the shimmering light and felt the familiar tingle that meant they were returning to their proper height.

Back in Brightley Meadow, the storm had eased. As the girls crossed the stream and headed for the wildlife hospital,

the rain suddenly stopped and the sun came out from behind the clouds.

"A rainbow!" cried Jess, pointing to a beautiful arch across the sky.

Mr Hart beckoned them from the barn door.

"Now the sun's shining," he said, "why don't you come and help me fix this nest box onto the chestnut tree for the three young squirrels you brought in. We'll keep an eye on them," he added.

"Choose a sunny spot," Mrs Hart called after them, "so the squirrels will be warm."

Lily and Jess exchanged a secret smile. They knew a whole family of squirrels who loved the sun!

The End

Grizelda and her dragons are trying to ruin the Rushy River boat race! Can Lily, Jess, and little hedgehog Emily Prickleback think of a way to stop them?

Find out in the next adventure,

Emily Prickleback's Clever Idea

Turn over for a sneak peek . . .

"Raaargh!"

Circling in the air was Dusty, Grizelda's yellow dragon!

The Pricklebacks seemed to be too frightened to move as the dragon gave a rasping giggle. "Heeheeheeheehee! I'm going to make it lovely and dry," she said. "Friendship Forest will be like a desert!"

Jess was horrified. "You can't do that!" she yelled. "What about the animals?"

"Heeheehee! Who cares about them?" said Dusty. "My yellow scales will look so pretty in the sun!"

Suddenly, she swooped lower.

"Oh no," cried Jess, "she's heading for the Pricklebacks!"

"Run!" shouted Lily.

"Hide!" yelled Goldie and Jess together.

But the Pricklebacks didn't move. They shook with fright, their spikes quivering.

Read

Emily Prickleback's Clever Idea

to find out what happens next!

Magic Animal Friends

Read all the Magic Animal Friends adventures and be part of the secret!

Series Two

COMING SOON!

Look out for
Jess and Lily's
next adventure:
Amelia Sparklepaw's Party
Problem

3 stories in 1!

www.magicanimalfriends.com

Puzzle Fun!

Can you spot the five differences between the two pictures of Sophie Flufftail?

ANSWERS

1. Extra leaves on the ground
2. Extra whisker
3. The frill is missing from her sleeve
4. Her eyebrow is missing
5. A stripe is missing from her top

Jess and Lily's Animal Facts

Lily and Jess love lots of different animals – both in Friendship Forest and in the real world.

Here are their top facts about

SQUIRRELS

like Sophie Flufftail

- Squirrels build homes called 'dreys'.
- Baby squirrels are called 'kittens'.
- Squirrels are very good at climbing and jumping, they can also swim!
- Squirrels store food by burying it in the ground ready for when there is less to eat in winter.
- Worldwide, there are over 265 species of squirrel. The African pygmy squirrel is the smallest at only 10cm from nose to tail. The Indian giant squirrel is the largest at a huge three feet long!

Tiggywinkles
Worlds Leading Wildlife Hospital

Lily's parents aren't the only ones who run a wildlife hospital.

Have you heard of Tiggywinkles – the world's busiest wildlife hospital? They take care of over 10,000 poorly animals every year and treat all kinds of wildlife, including hedgehogs, badgers, birds, foxes and deer.

If you are worried about a wild animal, you can have a look at their website for hints and tips about what to do.

www.tiggywinkles.com

Orchard Books supports Tiggywinkles.

Registered Charity No. 286447 Tiggywinkles,
Aston Road, Haddenham, Aylesbury,
Buckinghamshire HP17 8AF UK
Tel: 01844 292292
Email: mail@sttiggywinkles.org.uk